This book
belongs to

The Blue

The stories in this book were selected from the famous
BLUE FAIRY BOOK by Andrew Lang published by Longmans,
Green & Co., Inc.

Fairy Book

By
Andrew Lang

Illustrated by
Grace Dalles Clarke

Prepared under the supervision of
Josette Frank, Children's Book Adviser of the
Child Study Association of America.

RANDOM HOUSE · NEW YORK

The Princess on the Glass Hill

Once upon a time there was a man who had a meadow which lay on the side of a mountain, and in the meadow there was a barn in which he stored hay. But every St. John's Eve, when the grass in the meadow was at its height, it was all eaten up, just as if a flock of sheep had gnawed it down to the ground during the night. This happened once, and it happened twice. Then the man grew tired of losing his crop and said to his sons—he had three of them, and the third was called Cinderlad—that one of them must go and sleep in the barn on St. John's Eve, for it was absurd to let the grass be eaten up again, blade and stalk.

The eldest son was quite willing to go to the meadow; he would watch the grass, he said, and he would do it so well that neither man nor beast nor even the devil himself should have any of it. So he went to the barn and lay down to sleep, but when night was drawing near there was such a rumbling and such an earthquake that the walls and roof shook, and the lad jumped up and took to his heels. In the morning the grass had been all eaten and the barn remained empty that year as well.

Next St. John's Eve the second son was willing to show what he could do. He went to the barn and lay down to sleep, as his brother had, but when night was drawing near there was a great rumbling, and then an earthquake, which was even worse. When the youth heard it he was terrified and went off, running as if for his life.

The next year it was Cinderlad's turn, but when he made ready to go the others laughed at him and mocked him. "Well, you are just the right one to watch the hay, you who have never learned anything but how to sit among the ashes and bake yourself!" said they.

Cinderlad, however, did not trouble himself about what they said, but when evening drew near rambled away to the outlying field. He went into the barn and lay down, but in about an hour's time the rumbling and creaking began, and it was frightful to hear. "Well, if it gets no worse than that, I can stand it," said Cinderlad. In a little time the creaking began again, and the earth quaked so that all the hay flew about the boy.

"Oh, if it gets no worse than that I can stand it," said Cinderlad. But then came a third rumbling and a third earthquake, so violent the boy thought the walls and roof had fallen down. But when that was over everything suddenly grew as still as death around him. Cinderlad thought the rumbling would come again, but everything was quiet, and everything stayed quiet. When he had lain still a short time he heard something that sounded as if a horse were chewing just outside the barn door. He stole to the door to see what it was. A horse was standing there eating. It was such a big, fat and fine horse that Cinderlad had never seen one like it before; a saddle and bridle lay upon it, and a complete suit of armor for a knight, and everything was of copper and so bright that it shone.

"Ha, ha! It is you who eats our hay then," said the boy. "I will stop that." He quickly took out the steel that he used for striking fire, and threw it over the horse. Instantly it had no power to stir from the spot and became so tame the boy could do what he liked with it. So he mounted it and rode away to a place no one knew of but himself, and there he tied it up. When he came home again his brothers laughed and asked how he had got on.

"You did not lie long in the barn, or perhaps you did not even go so far as the field!" said they.

"I lay in the barn till the sun rose," said the boy. "God knows what there was to make you two so frightened."

"Well, we shall soon see whether you have watched the meadow or not," answered the brothers. But they found the grass was all standing just as long and as thick as it had been the night before.

The next St. John's Eve neither of the two brothers dared go to the outlying field to watch the crop, but Cinderlad went, and everything happened exactly as before. There was a rumbling and an earthquake, and then there was another, and then a third. But all three earthquakes were much, very much more violent then they had been before. Then everything became still as death again, and the boy heard something chewing outside the barn

door. Again there was a horse standing close by the wall of the house, eating and chewing, and it was far larger and fatter than the first horse, and it had a saddle on its back, and a bridle too, and a full suit of armor for a knight, all of bright silver.

"Ho, ho!" said the boy. "Is it you who eats our hay in the night? I will put a stop to that." So he took out his steel again and threw it over the horse's mane, and the beast stood there as quiet as a lamb. Then the boy rode this horse, too, away to the place where he kept the other and then went home again.

"I suppose you will tell us you have watched well this time," said the brothers.

"Well, so I have," said Cinderlad. Again the grass was standing as high and as thick as it had been before, but that did not make his brothers any kinder to Cinderlad.

When the third St. John's Eve came neither of the elder brothers dared lie in the outlying barn to watch the grass, for they had been so heartily frightened the night they had slept there they could not get over it. But Cinderlad went again. There were three earthquakes this time, each worse than the other, and the last flung the boy from one wall of the barn to the other; but then everything suddenly became still as death. When he had lain quietly a short time, he heard something chewing outside the barn door. And behold! A horse was standing just outside it, much larger and fatter than the two others he had caught. Its bridle and saddle were made of gold and there was a suit of golden armor, too.

"Ho, ho! It is you, then, who eats our hay this time," said the boy, "but I will put a stop to that." So again he pulled out his steel and threw it over the horse, and it stood as still as if it had been nailed to the field, and the boy could do what he liked with it. He mounted it and rode away to the place where he kept the two others, and then he went home again.

Now the two brothers mocked him just as they had done before. Cinderlad did not trouble himself about that, but bade them go to the field and see. This time, too, the grass was standing, looking as fine and as thick as ever.

Now in that country the king had proclaimed he would give his daughter to the one who could ride up to the top of a high, high hill of glass, slippery as ice, close to his palace. Upon the very top of this the king's daughter was to sit with three golden apples in her lap, and the man who could ride up and take the three golden apples should marry her and have half the kingdom. The king had this proclaimed through-out the whole kingdom, and in many other kingdoms, too.

The princess was very beautiful, and all who saw

her fell in love with her in spite of themselves. So all the princes and knights were eager to win her and half the kingdom besides. They came riding from the very ends of the world, dressed so splendidly their armor gleamed in the sunshine, and riding on horses which seemed to dance as they went. There was not one of these princes who did not think he was sure to win the princess.

When the day appointed came, there was such a crowd of knights and princes at the foot of the glass hill that they seemed to swarm, and everyone who could walk or even creep was there to see who would win the king's daughter. Cinderlad's two brothers were there too, but they would not hear of letting him go with them, for he was so dusty and grimy with sleeping among the ashes that they said everyone would laugh at them if they were seen in the company of such an oaf.

"Well, then, I will go all alone by myself," said Cinderlad.

When the two brothers arrived they saw that all the princes and knights were trying to ride up the glass hill and that their horses were in a foam. It was all in vain, for no sooner did the horses set foot upon the hill than down they slipped. Not once could they get up even so much as a few feet, for the hill was as smooth as a windowpane and as steep as the side of a house. But they were all eager to win the king's daughter and half the kingdom, so they rode and they slipped, and thus the contest went on. At last all the horses were so tired they could do no more, and the riders were forced to give up.

The king was just preparing to proclaim that the riding should begin afresh on the following day, when suddenly a knight came riding up on a horse so fine that no one had ever seen the like before. The knight had armor of copper, and his bridle was of copper too, and all his trappings were so bright that they shone. The other knights all called out to him that he might just as well spare himself the trouble of trying to ride up the glass hill. The new knight did not heed them, but rode straight off to the hill, and went up as if it were nothing at all. He rode for a long way—it may have been a third part of the way up—but then turned his horse around and rode down again.

The princess thought she had never yet seen such a handsome knight, and while he was riding up she thought to herself, "Oh, how I hope he may be able to come up to the top!" When she saw that he was turning his horse back she threw one of the golden apples down after him, and it rolled into his shoe. But when he reached the bottom of the hill he rode away so fast no one knew what had become of him.

So all the princes and knights were bidden to present themselves before the king that night so he who had ridden so far up the glass hill might show the golden apple which the king's daughter had thrown down. But no one had anything to show.

That night when Cinderlad's brothers came home they had a long story to tell. At first, they said, there was no one able to get even so much as one step up, but then came a knight who had armor of copper and bridle of copper, and his armor and trappings were so bright they shone to a great distance, and it was something of a sight to see him riding. He rode one third of the way up the glass hill, they said, and he could easily have ridden the whole of it if he had liked. But he had made up his mind that was enough for once.

"Oh, I should have liked to see him too, that I should," said Cinderlad.

Next day the brothers were for setting out again, and this time too

Cinderlad begged to go with them and see who rode. But no, they said he was not fit to do that, for he was much too ugly and dirty. "Well, well, then I will go all alone by myself," said Cinderlad. So the brothers went to the glass hill, and all the princes and knights began to ride again. Not one could even get so far as a yard up the hill. When they had tired out their horses so they could do no more, they again had to stop.

Just as the king was about to proclaim that the riding should take place next day for the last time so they might have one more chance, he suddenly thought it would be well to wait a little longer to see if the knight in copper armor would come on this day, too. Nothing was to be seen of him, but just as they were still looking for him, a knight came riding on a steed that was much, much finer than the one the knight in copper armor had ridden, and this knight had silver armor and a silver saddle and bridle, and all were so bright they shone and glistened when he was a long way off.

Again the other knights called to him and said he might just as well give up the attempt to ride up the glass hill, for it was useless to try. But the silver knight paid no heed to that and rode straight away to the glass hill, and went still farther up than the knight in copper armor had gone; but when he had ridden two thirds of the way up he turned his horse around, and rode down again.

The princess sat longing that he might be able to get up, and when she saw him turning back she threw the second apple after him, and it rolled into his shoe. As soon as he had reached the bottom of the glass hill he rode away so fast that no one could see what had become of him.

In the evening, when everyone was to appear before the king and princess, one knight went in after the other, but none of them had a golden apple to show.

That night the two brothers went home as they had done the night before, and told how things had gone and how everyone had ridden, but no one had been able to get up the hill.

"But last of all," they said, "came one in silver armor, and he had a silver bridle on his horse and a silver saddle, and oh, but he could ride! He took his horse two thirds of the way up the hill, but then he turned back. He was a fine fellow," said the brothers, "and the princess threw the second golden apple to him!"

"Oh, how I should have liked to see him, too!" said Cinderlad.

On the third day everything happened as on the former days. Everyone waited for the knight in silver armor, but he was neither to be seen nor heard of. At last, after a long time, came a knight riding upon a horse that was such a fine one its equal had never yet been seen. The knight had golden armor, and the horse a golden saddle and bridle, and these were all so bright they shone and dazzled everyone, even while the knight was still at a great distance. The other princes and knights did not think to call to him how useless it was to try, so amazed were they at the sight of his mag-

nificence. He rode straight away to the glass hill and galloped up as if it were no hill at all, and the princess had no time even to wish he might get up the whole way. As soon as he had ridden to the top, he took the third golden apple from the lap of the princess, and then turned his horse about and rode down again, and vanished from sight before anyone was able to say a word to him.

When the two brothers came home again that night, they had much to tell of how the riding had gone that day, and at last they told about the knight in the golden armor.

"He was a fine fellow! Such another splendid knight is not to be found on earth!" said the brothers.

"Oh, how I should have liked to see him, too!" said Cinderlad.

Next day all the knights and princes were to appear before the king and the princess so that he who had the golden apple might produce it. They all went in turn, first the princes, and then the knights, but none of them had a golden apple.

"But somebody must have it," said the king, "for with our own eyes we all saw a man ride up and take it." So he commanded that everyone in the kingdom should come to the palace and see if he could show the apple. And one after the other they all came, but no one had the golden apple, and after a long, long time Cinderlad's two brothers came likewise. They were the last of all, so the king inquired of them if there was no one else left in the kingdom to come.

"Oh, yes, we have a brother," said the two, "but he never got the golden apple! He never left the cinderheap on any of the three days."

"Never mind that," said the king. "As everyone else has come to the palace, let him come, too."

So Cinderlad was forced to go to the king's palace.

"Have you the golden apple?" asked the king.

"Yes, here is the first, and here is the second, and here is the third, too," said Cinderlad. And he took all three apples out of his pocket and with that threw off his sooty rags, and appeared there before them in his bright golden armor, which gleamed as he stood.

"You shall have my daughter, and half of my kingdom, and you have well earned both," said the king.

So Cinderlad married the king's daughter, and everyone made merry at the wedding. For all of them could make merry, even though they could not ride up the glass hill, and if they have not left off their merrymaking they must be at it still.

Puss in Boots

There was once a miller who, when he died, left to his three sons all that he had: his mill, his donkey, and his cat. The division was soon made. The eldest son had the mill, the second son the donkey, and the youngest nothing but the cat. The young fellow was quite sad at having so poor a lot.

"My brothers," said he, "may get their living handsomely enough by joining their stocks together. But for my part, when I have eaten my cat, and made me a muff of his skin, I must die of hunger."

The cat, who heard all this, said to him with a grave and serious air, "Do not worry, my good master. You need only give me a bag, and have a pair of boots made for me that I may scamper through the brambles. You shall see that you have not so bad a portion with me as you imagine."

The cat's master had often seen him play a great many cunning tricks to catch rats and mice; so he did not altogether despair. When the cat had what he asked for, he booted himself very gallantly, and putting his bag about his neck, he held the strings of it in his two forepaws and went into a warren where was a great abundance of rabbits. He put bran and lettuce into his bag and, stretching out full length as if dead, he waited for some young rabbits to come and rummage for what he had put into his bag.

Scarcely had he lain down than he had what he wanted: a rash and foolish young rabbit jumped into his bag. Mr. Puss, immediately drawing close the strings, killed him without pity. Proud of his prey, he went with it to the palace, and asked to speak with his majesty. He was shown into the king's apartment and, making a low bow, said to him:

"I have brought you, sir, a rabbit from the warren, which my noble lord, the Marquis of Carabas"—for that was the title Puss was pleased to give his master—"has commanded me to present to Your Majesty from him."

"Tell your master," said the king, "that I thank him, and that he gives me a great deal of pleasure."

Another time the cat hid himself among some standing corn, holding his bag open. When a brace of partridges ran into it, he drew the strings and so caught them both. He made a present of these to the king as he had the rabbit. The king, in like manner, received the partridges with great pleasure, and ordered some money to be given to Puss.

The cat continued thus for two or three months to carry game to his majesty from time to time. One day, when Puss knew for certain that the king was to take the air along the riverside with his daughter, the most beautiful princess in the world, he said to his master:

"If you will follow my advice your fortune is made. You have nothing to do but wash yourself in the river where I shall show you, and leave the rest to me."

The Marquis of Carabas did what the cat advised him to do, without knowing why or wherefore. While he was washing, the king passed by, and the cat began to cry out:

"Help! Help! My Lord Marquis of Carabas is going to be drowned."

At this the king put his head out of the coach window, and finding it was the cat who had so often brought him such good game, he commanded his guards to run immediately to the assistance of his lordship the Marquis of Carabas. While they were drawing him out of the river, the cat came up to the coach and told the king that, while his master was washing, there came by some rogues, who went off with his clothes, though he had cried out, "Thieves! Thieves!" several times, as loud as he could.

This cunning cat had hidden the clothes under a great stone. The king immediately commanded the officers of his wardrobe to run and fetch one of his best suits for the Marquis of Carabas.

17

The fine clothes set off his good looks, for he was well made and very handsome. The king's daughter took an immediate liking to him, and the Marquis of Carabas had no sooner cast two or three respectful and tender glances upon her than she fell in love with him. The king invited him to come into the coach and take the air with them. The cat, quite overjoyed to see his project begin to succeed, marched on in front and, meeting with some countrymen who were mowing a meadow, he said to them:

"Good people, you who are mowing, if you do not tell the king that the meadow you mow belongs to my Lord Marquis of Carabas, you shall be chopped as small as herbs for the pot."

The king did not fail to ask the mowers to whom the meadow belonged.

"To my Lord Marquis of Carabas," they answered all together, for the cat's threat had made them terribly afraid.

"You see, sir," said the marquis, "this is a meadow which never fails to yield a plentiful harvest every year."

Puss in Boots, who still went on in advance, met with some reapers, and said to them, "Good people, you who are reaping, if you do not tell the king that all this corn belongs to the Marquis of Carabas you shall be chopped as small as herbs for the pot."

The king, who passed by a moment after, wished to know to whom all that corn belonged.

"To my Lord Marquis of Carabas," replied the reapers, and the king was very well pleased with this answer, as well as with the marquis, whom he congratulated thereupon. Puss in Boots, who always went ahead, said the same words to all he met, and the king was astonished at the vast estates of the Marquis of Carabas.

Puss came at last to a stately castle, the master of which was an ogre, the richest ever known. All the lands which the king had then gone over belonged to this ogre. The cat, who had taken care to inform himself who this ogre was and what he could do, asked to speak with him, saying he could not pass so near his castle without paying his respects to him.

The ogre received him as civilly as an ogre could and bade him sit down.

"I have been assured," said the cat, "that you have the gift of being

able to change yourself into any sort of creature. You can, for example, transform yourself into a lion or elephant and the like."

"That is true," answered the ogre briskly, "and to convince you, you shall see me now become a lion."

Puss was so badly terrified at the sight of a lion so near him that he immediately got into the rain gutter. A little while after, when Puss saw that the ogre had resumed his natural form, he came down and confessed he had been very much frightened.

"I have also been informed," said the cat, "but I find it hard to believe, that you have the power to take on the shape of the smallest animal; for example, to change yourself into a rat or a mouse; but I must say I take this to be impossible."

"Impossible!" cried the ogre. "You shall see."

At the same time he changed himself into a mouse and began to run about the floor. Puss no sooner saw this than he fell upon him and ate him up.

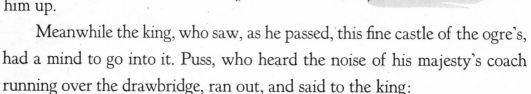

Meanwhile the king, who saw, as he passed, this fine castle of the ogre's, had a mind to go into it. Puss, who heard the noise of his majesty's coach running over the drawbridge, ran out, and said to the king:

"Your Majesty is welcome to this castle of my Lord Marquis of Carabas."

"What, my Lord Marquis!" cried the king. "And does this castle also belong to you? There can be nothing finer than this court and all the stately buildings which surround it. Let us go in, if you please."

The marquis gave his hand to the princess and followed the king, who went first. They passed into a spacious hall, where they found a magnificent feast which the ogre had prepared for his friends. They were due that very day to visit him, but dared not enter, knowing that the king was there. His majesty was charmed with the good qualities of the Lord Marquis of Carabas, as was his daughter, and seeing the vast estate he possessed, said to him:

"It will be owing to yourself only, my Lord Marquis, if you are not my son-in-law."

The marquis, making several low bows, accepted the honor which his majesty conferred upon him, and forthwith, that very same day, married the princess.

Puss became a great lord, and never ran after mice any more.

Hansel and Gretel

Once upon a time there dwelt on the outskirts of a large forest a poor wood-cutter with his wife and two children; the boy was called Hansel and the girl Gretel. The children's own mother had died and their father had brought home a new wife to care for them.

The woodcutter had always little enough to live on, and once, when there was a great famine in the land, he could not even provide his family with daily bread. One night, as he was tossing about in bed, full of cares and worry, he sighed and said to his wife:

"What is to become of us? How are we to support our poor children, now that we have nothing more for ourselves?"

"Early tomorrow morning," answered the woman, "we will take the children out into the thickest part of the wood. There we shall light a fire for them, give them each a piece of bread, and go on to our work, leaving them alone. They will not be able to find their way home, and we shall thus be rid of them."

"No, wife," said her husband, "that I won't do. How could I find it in my heart to leave my children alone in the wood? The wild beasts would come and tear them to pieces."

"Oh," said she, "then we must all four die of hunger, and you may just as well go and plane the boards for our coffins." And she left him no peace till he consented.

"But I cannot help feeling sorry for the poor children," added the husband.

The children, too, had not been able to sleep for hunger, and had heard what their stepmother had said to their father. Gretel wept bitterly while she said to Hansel, "Now we are done for."

"No, no, Gretel," said Hansel, "don't fret yourself. I will find a way of escape, never fear."

When the old people had fallen asleep he got up, slipped on his little coat, opened the back door and stole out. The moon was shining clearly, and the white pebbles which lay in front of the house glittered like bits of silver. Hansel bent down and filled his pocket with as many of them as he could. Then he went back and said to Gretel:

"Be comforted, dear little sister, and go to sleep. God will not desert us." And he lay down in bed again.

At daybreak, even before the sun was up, the woman came and woke the two children. "Get up, you lie-abeds," she said. "We are all going to the forest to fetch wood."

She gave them each a bit of bread and said, "There's something for your luncheon, but do not eat it before, for it is all you will get."

Gretel took the bread under her apron, as Hansel had the stones in his pocket. Then they all set out together on the way to the forest. After they had walked for a little, Hansel stood still and

looked back at the house, and this he did again and again.

His father observed him, and asked, "Hansel, what are you gazing at, and why do you always remain behind? Take care, and do not lose your footing."

"Oh, Father," said Hansel, "I am looking back at my white kitten, which is sitting on the roof waving me a farewell."

The woman exclaimed, "What a donkey you are! That isn't your kitten, that is the morning sun shining on the chimney."

Actually Hansel had not looked back at his kitten, but had dropped one of the white pebbles out of his pocket onto the path.

When they had reached the middle of the forest the father said, "Now, children, go and fetch a lot of wood, and I will light a fire."

Hansel and Gretel heaped up brushwood till they made a pile nearly the size of a small hill. The brushwood was set alight, and when the flames leaped high the woman said:

"Now lie down by the fire, children, and rest yourselves. We are going into the forest to cut wood; when we have finished we will come back and fetch you."

Hansel and Gretel sat down beside the fire, and at midday ate their little bits of bread. They heard the strokes of the axe, so they thought their father was quite near. However, it was no axe they heard, but a bough on a dead tree blown about by the wind. And when they had sat for a long time their eyes closed with fatigue, and they fell fast asleep. When they awoke at last it was pitch dark.

Gretel began to cry, and said, "How are we ever to get out of the wood?"

But Hansel comforted her. "Wait a bit," he said, "till the moon is up, and then we will find our way sure enough."

And when the full moon had risen he took his sister by the hand and followed the pebbles, which shone like new pennies and showed them the path. They walked all through the night, and at daybreak reached their father's house again. They knocked at the door, and when the woman opened it, she exclaimed:

"You naughty children, what a time you have slept in the wood! We thought you were never coming back." But the father rejoiced, for his conscience had reproached him for leaving his children.

Not long afterward there was again a great famine in the land, and the children heard the woman say, "Everything is eaten up once more; we have only half a loaf of bread in the house. We shall lead them deeper into the wood this time so they cannot find their way out again."

The man's heart smote him heavily, and he said, "Surely it would be better to share the last bite with one's children!" But he finally agreed to do as his wife said.

When the old people were asleep Hansel wanted to go out and pick up pebbles again, as he had done the first time; but the woman had barred the door, and he could not get out. He consoled his little sister, and said, "Don't cry, Gretel. Sleep peacefully, for God is sure to help us."

At early dawn the woman came and made the children get up. They received their bit of bread, but it was even smaller than the time before. On the way to the wood Hansel crumbled it in his pocket, and every few minutes he stood still and dropped a crumb on the ground.

"Hansel, why are you stopping and looking about you?" said the father.

"I'm looking back at my little pigeon, which is sitting on the roof waving me a farewell," answered Hansel.

The woman led the children still deeper into the forest, farther than they had ever been before. Then a big fire was lit again, and she said:

"Just sit down, children, and if you are tired you can sleep a bit. We are going into the forest to cut wood and in the evening shall come back to fetch you."

At midday Gretel divided her bread with Hansel, for he had strewed his all along their path. Then they fell asleep, and evening passed away, but nobody came for the poor children. They did not awake till it was pitch

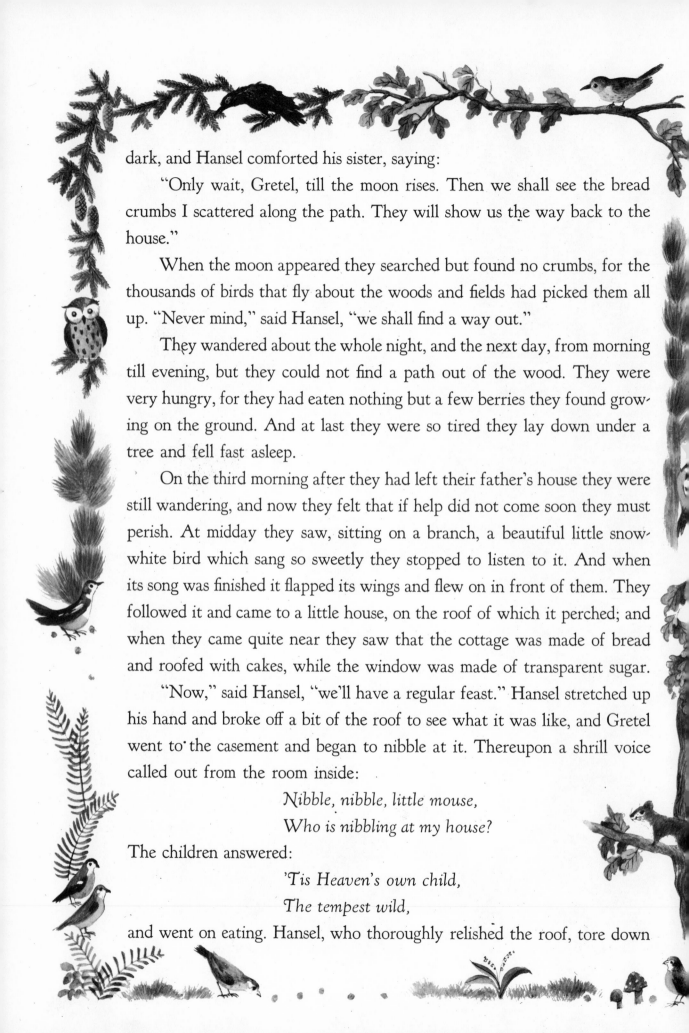

dark, and Hansel comforted his sister, saying:

"Only wait, Gretel, till the moon rises. Then we shall see the bread crumbs I scattered along the path. They will show us the way back to the house."

When the moon appeared they searched but found no crumbs, for the thousands of birds that fly about the woods and fields had picked them all up. "Never mind," said Hansel, "we shall find a way out."

They wandered about the whole night, and the next day, from morning till evening, but they could not find a path out of the wood. They were very hungry, for they had eaten nothing but a few berries they found grow-ing on the ground. And at last they were so tired they lay down under a tree and fell fast asleep.

On the third morning after they had left their father's house they were still wandering, and now they felt that if help did not come soon they must perish. At midday they saw, sitting on a branch, a beautiful little snow-white bird which sang so sweetly they stopped to listen to it. And when its song was finished it flapped its wings and flew on in front of them. They followed it and came to a little house, on the roof of which it perched; and when they came quite near they saw that the cottage was made of bread and roofed with cakes, while the window was made of transparent sugar.

"Now," said Hansel, "we'll have a regular feast." Hansel stretched up his hand and broke off a bit of the roof to see what it was like, and Gretel went to the casement and began to nibble at it. Thereupon a shrill voice called out from the room inside:

> *Nibble, nibble, little mouse,*
> *Who is nibbling at my house?*

The children answered:

> *'Tis Heaven's own child,*
> *The tempest wild,*

and went on eating. Hansel, who thoroughly relished the roof, tore down

a big bit of it, while Gretel pushed out a whole round windowpane, and sat down the better to enjoy it. Suddenly the door opened, and an old woman leaning on a staff hobbled out. Hansel and Gretel were so terrified that they let fall what they had in their hands. But the old woman shook her head and said:

"Oh, ho, you dear children! Who led you here? Just come in and stay with me. No harm shall befall you." She took them both by the hand and led them into the house and laid a sumptuous dinner before them—milk and sugared pancakes, with apples and nuts. After they had eaten, two beautiful little white beds were prepared for them, and when Hansel and Gretel lay down in them they felt as if they were in Heaven.

The old woman had appeared to be most friendly, but she was really an old witch. When anyone came into her power she cooked and ate the person and held a regular feast day. Now witches have red eyes and cannot see far but, like beasts, they have a keen sense of smell and know when human beings pass by. When Hansel and Gretel fell into her hands she laugh maliciously and said, "I have them now. They cannot escape me."

Early in the morning, before the children were awake, she rose, and when she saw them both sleeping so peacefully, with their round rosy cheeks, she muttered to herself, "That will be a dainty bite." Then she seized Hansel with her bony hand and carried him into a little stable, and barred the door on him. He might scream as much as he liked, it did him no good.

Then the witch went to Gretel, shook her till she awoke, and cried, "Get up, you lazybones, fetch water and cook something for your brother. When he is fat I shall eat him." Gretel began to cry bitterly, but it was of no use; she had to do what the wicked witch bade her.

So the best food was cooked for poor Hansel, but Gretel got nothing but crab shells. Every morning the old woman hobbled out to the stable and cried, "Hansel, put out your finger that I may feel if you are getting

fat." But Hansel always stretched out a bone, and the old woman, whose eyes were dim, could not see it and, thinking always that it was Hansel's finger, wondered why he fattened so slowly.

When four weeks had passed and Hansel still remained thin, the witch lost patience and determined to wait no longer. "Hi! Gretel," she called to the girl, "be quick and get some water. Whether Hansel is fat or thin, I'm going to cook him tomorrow."

Oh, how the poor little sister sobbed as she carried the water, and how the tears rolled down her cheeks! "Kind Heaven help us now!" she cried. "If only the wild beasts in the wood had eaten us, then at least we should have died together."

"Just hold your peace," said the old witch. "Nothing can help you now."

Early in the morning Gretel had to go out and hang up the kettle full of water and light the fire. "First we shall bake," said the old dame. "I have heated the oven and kneaded the dough." She pushed Gretel out to the oven, from which fiery flames were already issuing. "Creep in," said the witch, "and see if it is properly heated so we can shove in the bread." For when she had Gretel in the oven she meant to close the door and let the girl bake that she might eat her up too.

But Gretel realized what she intended to do, and said, "I do not know how I am to do it. How do I get in?"

"You silly goose," said the witch, "the opening is big enough. See, I could get in myself," and she crawled toward it and poked her head into the oven. Then Gretel gave her a shove that sent her right in, shut the iron door, and drew the bolt. Gracious! How the witch yelled! It was quite horrible, but Gretel fled, and the wretched old woman was left to perish miserably.

Gretel flew straight to Hansel, opened the little stable door, and cried, "Hansel, we are free; the old witch is dead." Then Hansel sprang like a bird out of a cage when the door is opened. How they rejoiced and fell on each other's necks and jumped for joy and kissed one another! As they no longer had any cause for fear, they went into the witch's house, and there they found, in every corner of the room, boxes with pearls and precious stones.

"These are even better than pebbles," said Hansel, and crammed his pockets full of them.

"I too will bring something home," said Gretel. And she filled her apron full.

"But now," said Hansel, "let us go well away from the witch's wood." When they had wandered about for some hours they came to a big lake.

"We cannot get over," said Hansel. "I see no bridge of any kind."

"Yes, and there is no ferryboat either," answered Gretel. "But look, there swims a white duck; if I ask her she will help us." And she called out:

Here are two children, mournful very,
Seeing neither bridge nor ferry;
Take us upon your downy white back,
And row us over, quack, quack, quack!

The duck swam toward them, and Hansel got on her back and bade his little sister sit beside him. "No," answered Gretel, "we should be too heavy a load for the duck. She shall carry us across separately." The good bird did this, and when they were landed safely on the other side and had gone on for a while, the wood became more and more familiar to them, and at length they saw their father's house in the distance. Then they set off at a run, and bounding into the room fell on their father's neck.

The man had not passed a happy hour since he had left them in the wood, but the woman had died. Gretel shook out her apron and the pearls and precious stones rolled about the room, and Hansel threw down one handful after another out of his pocket. Thus all their troubles were ended, and they all lived happily ever afterward.

Felicia and the Pot of Pinks

Once upon a time there was a poor laborer who, feeling he had not much longer to live, wished to divide his possessions between his son and daughter, whom he loved dearly. So he called them to him, and said:

"Your mother brought me as her dowry two stools, a straw bed and a hen. I have, besides, a pot of pinks and a silver ring, which were given me by a noble lady who once lodged in my poor cottage. When she went away she said to me:

" 'Be careful of my gifts, good man; see that you do not lose the ring or forget to water the pinks. As for your daughter, I promise you she shall be more beautiful than anyone you ever saw. Call her Felicia, and when she grows up give her the ring and the pot of pinks to console her for her poverty.' Take them both then, my dear child," he added, "and your brother shall have everything else."

The two children seemed quite contented, and when their father died they wept for him and divided his possessions as he had told them. Felicia believed her brother loved her, but when she sat down upon one of the stools he said angrily:

"Keep your pot of pinks and your ring, but let my things alone. I like order in my house."

Felicia, who was very gentle, said nothing but stood up, crying quietly, while Bruno, her brother, sat comfortably by the fire. When suppertime came, Bruno had a delicious egg, and he threw the shell to Felicia, saying:

"There, that is all I can give you. If you don't like it, go out and catch frogs; there are plenty of them in the marsh close by."

Felicia went away to her own little room. She found it filled with the sweet scent of the pinks, and going up to them, she said sadly:

"Beautiful pinks, you are so sweet and so pretty, you are the only comfort I have left. You may be very sure I will take care of you and water you well, and never allow any cruel hand to tear you from your stems."

As she leaned over them she noticed they were very dry. So, taking her pitcher, she ran off in the clear moonlight to the fountain. She was about to sit down upon the brink to rest when she saw a stately lady coming toward her, surrounded by many attendants. Six maids of honor carried her train, and she leaned upon the arm of another.

When they came near the fountain a canopy was spread for her, under which was placed a sofa of cloth-of-gold, and presently a dainty supper was served upon a table covered with dishes of gold and crystal, while the wind in the trees and the falling water of the fountain murmured the softest music.

Felicia was hidden in the shade, too much astonished by all she saw to venture to move. But in a few moments the queen said, "I fancy I see a shepherdess near that tree. Bid her come hither."

So Felicia came forward and saluted the queen timidly, but with so much grace that all were surprised.

"What are you doing here, my pretty child?" asked the queen. "Are you not afraid of robbers?"

"Ah, madam," said Felicia, "a poor shepherdess who has nothing to lose does not fear robbers."

"You are not rich, then?" said the queen, smiling.

"I am so poor," answered Felicia, "that a pot of pinks and a silver ring are my only possessions in the world."

"But you have a heart," said the queen. "What would you say if anybody wanted to steal that?"

"I do not know what it is like to lose one's heart, madam," Felicia replied. "But I have always heard that without a heart one cannot live, and if it is broken one must die. In spite of my poverty I should be sorry not to live."

"You are quite right to take care of your heart, pretty one," said the queen. "But tell me, have you had supper?"

"No, madam," answered Felicia.

Then the queen ordered a place to be made for her at the table, and herself filled Felicia's plate with good things.

"What were you doing at the fountain so late?" said the queen.

"I came to fetch water for my pinks, madam," the girl answered, stooping to pick up the pitcher which stood beside her. But when she showed it to the queen she was amazed to see it had turned to gold, all sparkling with great diamonds, and the water, which filled it, was more fragrant than the sweetest roses. She was afraid to take it until the queen said:

"It is yours, Felicia. Go and water your pinks with it, and let it remind you that the Queen of the Woods is your friend."

The shepherdess threw herself at the queen's feet, and thanked her for her gracious words. "Ah, madam," she cried, "if I might beg you to stay here a moment I would run and fetch my pot of pinks for you—they could not fall into better hands."

"Go, Felicia," said the queen, stroking her cheek softly. "I will wait here until you come back."

So Felicia took up her pitcher and ran to her little room. But while she had been away Bruno had taken the pot of pinks, leaving a great cabbage in its place. Felicia was much distressed, and did not know what to do. But at last she ran back to the fountain and, kneeling before the queen, said:

"Madam, Bruno has taken my pot of pinks, so I have nothing but my silver ring. I beg you to accept it as proof of my gratitude."

"But if I take your ring, my pretty shepherdess," said the queen, "you will have nothing left. What will you do then?"

"Ah, madam," she answered simply, " if I have your friendship I shall do very well."

So the queen took the ring and, putting it on her finger, mounted her chariot, which was made of coral studded with emeralds, and drawn by six

milk-white horses. Felicia looked after her until the winding of the forest path hid her from sight, and then she went back to the cottage, thinking over all the wonderful things that had happened.

The first thing she did when she reached her room was to throw the cabbage out of the window. But she was surprised to hear an odd little voice cry out, "Oh, I am half killed!" She could not tell where it came from, because cabbages do not generally speak.

As soon as it was light Felicia, who was very unhappy about the loss of her pot of pinks, went out to look for it, and the first thing she found was the unfortunate cabbage. She gave it a push with her foot, saying:

"What are you doing here, and how dare you put yourself in the place of my pot of pinks?"

"If I hadn't been carried," replied the cabbage, "you may be very
sure I should not have thought of
going there."

It made Felicia shiver with
fright to hear the cabbage talk, but
he went on, "If you will be good
enough to plant me by my comrades
again, I can tell you where your
pinks are at this moment—hidden in
Bruno's bed!"

Felicia was in despair when
she heard this, not knowing how
she was to get them back. But she
replanted the cabbage very kindly in
his old place, and as she finished
doing it, she saw Bruno's hen.
Catching hold of it, she said:

"Come here, horrid little creature! You shall suffer for all the
unkind things my brother has done to me."

"Ah, shepherdess," said the hen, "do not kill me. I am rather a gossip and I can tell you some surprising things you will like to hear. Do not imagine you are the daughter of the poor laborer who brought you up. Your mother was a queen who had six girls already, and the king threatened that unless she had a son who could inherit his kingdom she would have her head cut off."

"So when the queen had another little daughter she was frightened and agreed with her friend, who was a fairy, to exchange her for the fairy's son. Now the queen had been shut up in a great tower by the king's orders, and when a great many days went by and still she heard nothing from the fairy she made her escape from the window by means of a rope ladder, taking her baby with her. After wandering about until she was half dead with cold and fatigue she reached this cottage. I was the laborer's wife and was a good nurse, and the queen gave you into my charge. She told me all her misfortunes, but died before she had time to say what was to become of you.

"As I never could keep a secret, I could not help telling this strange tale to my neighbors, and one day a beautiful lady came here and I told it to her also. When I had finished she touched me with a wand she held in her hand and instantly I became a hen, and there was an end of my talking! I was very sad, and my husband, who was out when it happened, never knew what had become of me. After seeking me everywhere he believed I must have been drowned or eaten by wild beasts in the forest.

"That same lady came here once more and commanded that you should be called Felicia, and she left the ring and the pot of pinks to be given to you. While she was in the house twenty-five of the king's guards came to search for you, doubtless meaning to kill you, but she muttered a few words and immediately they all turned into cabbages. It was one of them you threw out of your window yesterday. I do not know how it was he could speak—I have never heard any of them say a word before, nor have I been able to do it myself until now."

The princess was greatly astonished at the hen's story, and said kindly, "I am truly sorry for you, my poor nurse, and wish it were in my power to restore you to your real form. But we must not despair. Something must be going to happen soon."

Bruno had gone out into the forest, never thinking that Felicia would search in his room for the pinks. As soon as she entered she saw a terrible army of rats, who were guarding the straw bed. When she approached it they sprang at her, biting and scratching furiously.

Quite terrified, she drew back, crying out, "Oh, my dear pinks, how can you stay here in such bad company?"

Then she suddenly bethought herself of the pitcher of water. Hoping it might have some magic power, she ran to fetch it and sprinkled a few drops over the fierce-looking swarm of rats. In a moment not a tail or a whisker was to be seen. Each one had made for his hole as fast as his legs could carry

him, and Felicia could safely take her pot of pinks. She found them nearly dying for want of water, and hastily poured all that was left in the pitcher upon them. As she bent over them, enjoying their delicious scent, a soft voice that seemed to rustle among the leaves said:

"Lovely Felicia, the day has come at last when I may have the happiness of telling you how even the flowers love you and rejoice in your beauty."

The princess, quite overcome by the strangeness of hearing a cabbage, a hen and a pink speak, and by the sight of an army of rats, suddenly became very pale and fainted away.

At this moment Bruno came in. Working hard in the heat had not improved his temper, and when he saw that Felicia had succeeded in finding her pinks he was so angry he dragged her out into the garden and shut the door upon her. The fresh air soon made her open her eyes, and there before her stood the Queen of the Woods, looking as charming as ever.

"You have a bad brother," she said. "I saw how cruelly he turned you out. Shall I punish him for it?"

"Ah, no, madam," Felicia said. "I am not angry with him."

"Ah, dear child," said the queen, "the way you speak assures me that you are indeed a real princess, and I can save you from being treated in such a way again."

She was interrupted at this moment by the arrival of a very handsome young man. He wore a coat of green velvet fastened with emerald clasps, and had a crown of pinks on his head. He knelt upon one knee and kissed the queen's hand.

"Ah," she cried, "my pink, my dear son, what happiness to see you restored to your natural shape by Felicia's aid!" She embraced him joyfully, and then turning to Felicia she said:

"Charming Princess, I know all the hen has told you, but you cannot have heard that the winds, who were to carry my son to the tower where the queen, your mother, so anxiously awaited him, left him instead in a garden of flowers. Whereupon a fairy, with whom I had quarreled, changed him into a pink, and I could do nothing to prevent it.

"You may imagine how angry I was, and how I tried to find some means of undoing the mischief she had done; but there was no help for it. I could only bring my son to the place where you were being brought up, hoping he might love you when you grew up, and by your care be restored to his natural form. And you see everything has come right, as I hoped it would. Your giving me the silver ring was the sign that the power of the charm was nearly over, and my enemy's last chance was to frighten you with her army of rats. Now, my dear Felicia, if you will be married to my son with this silver ring your future happiness is certain. Do you think him handsome and amiable enough to be willing to marry him?"

"Madam," replied Felicia, flushing, "you overwhelm me with your kindness. I know you are my mother's friend, and that by your art you turned the soldiers, who were sent to kill me, into cabbages, and my nurse into a hen, and you do me only too much honor in proposing that I shall marry your son. How can I explain to you the cause of my hesitation? I feel, for the first time in my life, how happy it would make me to be beloved. Can you indeed give me the prince's heart?"

"It is yours already, lovely Princess!" he cried, taking her hand in his. "But for the horrible enchantment which kept me silent I should have told you long ago how dearly I love you."

This made the princess very happy, and the queen, who could not bear to see her dressed as a poor shepherdess, touched her with her wand, saying, "I wish you to be attired as befits your rank and beauty." Immediately the princess' cotton dress became a magnificent robe of silver brocade, and her soft dark hair was encircled by a crown of diamonds, from which floated a clear white veil. With her bright eyes, and the charming color in her cheeks, she was altogether so dazzling the prince could hardly bear it.

"How pretty you are, Felicia!" he cried. "Don't keep me in suspense, I entreat you; say that you will marry me."

"Ah," said the queen smiling, "I think she will not refuse."

Just then Bruno, who was going back to his work, came out of the cottage, and thought he must be dreaming when he saw Felicia. But she called to him kindly and begged the queen to take pity on him.

"What," she said, "when he was so unkind to you?"

"Ah, madam," said the princess, "I am so happy I should like everybody else to be happy too."

The queen kissed her, and said, "Well, to please you, let me see what I can do for this cross Bruno." And with a wave of her wand she turned the poor little cottage into a splendid palace, full of treasures; only the two stools and the straw bed remained just as they were, to remind him of his former poverty. Then the queen touched Bruno himself and made him gentle and polite and grateful, and he thanked her and the princess a thousand times. Lastly, the queen restored the hen and the cabbages to their natural forms, and left them all very contented.

The prince and the princess were married as soon as possible with great splendor, and lived happily ever after.

Jack the Giant Killer

In the reign of the famous King Arthur there lived in Cornwall a lad named Jack, who was a boy of bold temper and took delight in hearing or reading of conjurers, giants and fairies. He used to listen eagerly to the deeds of the knights of King Arthur's Round Table.

In those days there lived on St. Michael's Mount, off Cornwall, a huge giant, eighteen feet high and nine feet round. His fierce and savage looks were the terror of all who beheld him.

Cormoran, as the giant was called, dwelt in a gloomy cavern on the top of the mountain, and used to wade over to the mainland in search of prey. He would capture and throw half a dozen oxen upon his back, tie three times as many sheep and hogs around his waist, and then march back to his cavern. The giant had done this for many years when Jack resolved to destroy him.

One winter's evening Jack took a horn, a shovel, a pickaxe, his armor and a dark lantern, and went to the mount. There he dug a pit twenty-two feet deep and twenty feet broad. He covered the top over to make it look like solid ground. Then he blew such a blast that the giant awoke and came out of his den, crying out:

"You saucy villain, you shall pay for this. I shall broil you for my breakfast."

He had just spoken when, taking one step farther, he tumbled head-long into the pit, and Jack struck him a blow on the head with his pickaxe which killed him. Jack then returned home to cheer his friends with the news.

Another giant, called Blunderbore, vowed to be revenged on Jack if ever he should have him in his power. This giant kept an enchanted castle in the midst of a lonely wood. Some time after the death of Cormoran, Jack was passing through a wood and, being weary, sat down and went to sleep.

The giant, passing by and seeing Jack, carried him off to his castle, where he locked him up in a large room, the floor of which was covered with the skulls and bones of men and women. Soon after he went to fetch his brother, who was likewise a giant, to take a meal off Jack. Through the bars of his prison, Jack saw the two giants approaching.

Perceiving in one corner of the room a strong cord, Jack took courage and, making a slipknot at each end, he threw the cord over the giants' heads and tied it to the window bars. He then pulled till he had choked them. Then he slid down the rope and stabbed them to the heart.

Jack next took a great bunch of keys from the pocket of Blunderbore and went into the castle again. He made a thorough search of all the rooms, and in one of them found three ladies tied up by the hair of their heads and almost starved to death. They told him their husbands had been killed by the giants, who had then condemned them to be starved to death.

"Ladies," said Jack, "I have put an end to the monster and his wicked brother. I give you this castle and all the riches it contains, to make some amends for the dreadful pain you have felt."

He then very politely gave them the keys of the castle and went farther on his journey to Wales. As Jack had but little money, he went on as fast as possible. At length he came to a handsome house and knocked at the door, which was opened by a Welsh giant. Jack said he was a traveler who had lost his way. On hearing this the giant made him welcome, and led him into a room where there was a good bed.

Jack took off his clothes quickly, but though he was weary he could not sleep. Soon after this he heard the giant walking backward and forward in the next room, and saying to himself:

> Though here you lodge with me this night,
> You shall not see the morning light;
> My club shall dash your brains out quite.

Say you so? thought Jack. So these are your tricks upon travelers? But I hope to prove as cunning as you are. Then, getting out of bed, he groped about the room, and at last found a large thick log. He laid it in his own place in the bed and then hid himself in a dark corner of the room.

The giant, about midnight, entered the apartment, and with his bludgeon struck many blows on the bed, in the very place where Jack had laid the log. Then he went back to his own room, thinking he had broken all Jack's bones.

Early in the morning Jack put a bold face upon the matter and walked into the giant's room to thank him for his lodging. The giant started when he saw him and began to stammer:

"Oh dear me; is it you? Pray, how did you sleep last night? Did you hear or see anything in the dead of the night?"

"Nothing worth speaking of," said Jack carelessly. "A rat, I believe, gave me three or four slaps with his tail and disturbed me a little. But I soon went to sleep again."

The giant wondered more and more at this, yet he did not answer a word, but went to bring two great bowls of hasty-pudding for their breakfast. Jack wanted it to appear that he could eat as much as the giant, so he hid a leather bag inside his coat and slipped the hasty-pudding into this bag while seeming to put it into his mouth. When breakfast was over he said to the giant:

"Now I will show you a fine trick. I can cure all wounds with a touch. I could cut off my head in one minute, and the next put it sound again on my shoulders. You shall see an example." He then took hold of a knife, ripped up the leather bag, and all the hasty-pudding tumbled out upon the floor.

"Ods splutter hur nails!" cried the Welsh giant, who was ashamed to be outdone by such a little fellow as Jack. "Hur can do that hurself!" So he snatched up the knife, plunged it into his own stomach, and in a moment dropped down dead.

Having thus far been successful in all his undertakings, Jack resolved not to be idle in future. He therefore furnished himself with a horse, a cap of knowledge, a sword of sharpness, shoes of swiftness and an invisible coat, the better to perform the wonderful enterprises that lay before him.

He traveled over high hills, and on the third day he came to a large and spacious forest through which his road lay. Scarcely had he entered the forest when he beheld a monstrous giant dragging along by the hair of their heads a handsome knight and his lady. Jack alighted from his horse and, tying him to an oak tree, put on his invisible coat, under which he carried his sword of sharpness.

When he came up to the giant he plunged his sword into the giant's body and killed him.

The knight and his lady thanked Jack for their deliverance, and invited him to their house to receive a proper reward for his services. "No," said Jack,

"I cannot be easy till I find out where this monster lived." So, taking the knight's directions, he mounted his horse and soon after came in sight of another giant, who was sitting on a block of timber waiting for his brother's return.

Jack alighted from his horse and, putting on his invisible coat, approached and aimed a blow at the giant's head. But he missed his aim and cut off only the giant's nose. At this the giant seized his club and laid about him most unmercifully.

"Nay," said Jack, "if this be the case I'd better dispatch you!" So he stabbed him to death.

Jack then proceeded on his journey and traveled over hills and dales until, arriving at the foot of a high mountain, he knocked at the door of a lonely house, where an old man let him in. When Jack was seated the

hermit said to him:

"My son, on the top of this mountain is an enchanted castle, kept by the giant Galligantus and a vile magician. They seized a duke's daughter as she was walking in her father's garden and brought her here transformed into a deer."

Jack promised that in the morning, at the risk of his life, he would break the enchantment. After a sound sleep he rose early, put on his invisible coat, and made ready for the attempt.

When he had climbed to the top of the mountain he saw two fiery monsters; but he passed between them without the least fear of danger, for they could not see him because of his invisible coat. On the castle gate he found a golden trumpet, under which were written these lines:

> *Whoever can this trumpet blow*
> *Shall cause the giant's overthrow.*

As soon as Jack had read this he seized the trumpet and blew a shrill

blast, which made the gates fly open and the very castle itself tremble.

The giant and the magician now knew their wicked lives were at an end, and they stood biting their thumbs and shaking with fear. Jack with his sword of sharpness soon killed the giant; and the magician was then carried away by a whirlwind; and all the knights and beautiful ladies who had been changed into birds and beasts returned to their proper shapes. The castle vanished away like smoke, and the head of the giant Galligantus was then sent to King Arthur.

The knights and ladies rested that night at the old man's hermitage, and next day they set out for the court. Jack went up to the king and gave his majesty an account of all his fierce battles.

Jack's fame had now spread through the whole country, and at the king's desire the duke gave him his daughter in marriage, to the joy of all his kingdom. After this the king gave him a large estate, on which he and his lady lived the rest of their days in joy and contentment.

Toads and Diamonds

There was once upon a time a widow who had two daughters. The elder was so much like her in face and disposition that whoever looked upon the daughter saw the mother. They were both so disagreeable and so proud there was no living with them.

The younger, who was the very picture of her father for courtesy and sweetness of temper, was one of the most beautiful girls ever seen. As people naturally love their own likeness, this mother doted on her elder daughter, and at the same time did not care at all for the younger. She made her eat in the kitchen and work continually.

Among other things, this poor child was forced twice a day to draw water from a fountain a mile and a half from the house and bring home a pitcher full of it. One day, when she was at this fountain, there came to her a poor woman who begged of her to let her drink.

"Oh, ay, with all my heart, Goody," said this pretty girl. And immediately rinsing the pitcher, she took up some water from the clearest place of the fountain and gave it to her, holding up the pitcher all the while so that she might drink more easily.

After the good woman had drunk all she wanted, she said to her, "You are so very pretty, my dear, so good and so mannerly, I cannot help giving you a gift." For this was a fairy, who had taken the form of a poor countrywoman to see how kind this pretty girl would be. "My gift to you will be," continued the fairy, "that, at every word you speak, there shall come out of your mouth either a flower or a jewel."

When this pretty girl came home her mother scolded her for staying so long at the fountain.

"I beg your pardon, Mamma," said the poor girl, "for not making more haste." And in speaking these words there came out of her mouth five roses, three pearls and two diamonds.

"What is it I see there?" said her mother, astonished. "I think I see pearls and diamonds come out of the girl's mouth! How did this come about, child?"

This was the first time she had ever called her "child."

The poor girl told her frankly all that had happened, and while she spoke great numbers of diamonds dropped from her mouth.

"In good faith," cried the mother, "I must send my elder child there. Come, look what comes out of your sister's mouth when she speaks. Would you not be glad, my dear, to have the same gift given to you? You have nothing to do but draw water out of the fountain, and when a certain poor woman asks you to let her drink, to give it to her very courteously."

"It would be a fine sight indeed," said this ill-bred minx, "to see me draw water."

"You shall go, hussy," said the mother, "and this minute."

So she went, but grumbling all the way, taking with her the best silver tankard in the house. She was no sooner at the fountain than she saw coming out of the wood a lady most gloriously dressed, who came up to her and asked to drink. This was the very fairy who had appeared to her sister, but had now taken the air and dress of a princess, to see how far this girl's rudeness would go.

"Am I come hither," said the proud, saucy girl, "to serve you with water, pray? I suppose the silver tankard was brought for your ladyship? However, you may drink out of it, if you have a fancy."

"You are not very well mannered," answered the fairy. "Well, then, since you have so little breeding and are so disobliging, my gift to you is that at every word you speak there shall come out of your mouth a snake or a toad."

As soon as her mother saw her coming she cried out, "Well, daughter?"

"Well, mother?" answered the pert hussy, throwing out of her mouth a viper and a toad.

"Oh, mercy!" cried the mother. "What is it I see? Oh, it is that wretch your sister who is to blame for all this, but she shall pay for it."

And immediately she ran to beat her.

The poor child fled away from her and went to hide herself in the forest. The king's son, then on his return from hunting, met her and, seeing her so pretty, asked what she did there alone and why she cried.

"Alas, sir, my mother has turned me out of doors."

The king's son, who saw five or six pearls and as many diamonds come out of her mouth, asked her to tell him how that happened. She thereupon told him the whole story. The king's son fell in love with her, and conducted her to the palace of the king his father, and there married her.

As for the proud elder sister, she soon made herself so much hated that nobody would have anything to do with her.

Why the Sea is Salt

Once upon a time, long, long ago, there were two brothers, the one rich and the other poor. When Christmas Eve came, the poor one had not a bite in the house, either of meat or bread; so he went to his brother, and begged him, in God's name, to give him something for Christmas Day. It was by no means the first time his brother had been forced to give some food to him, and he was no better pleased at being asked now than he generally was.

"If you will do what I ask you, you shall have a whole ham," said he. The poor one immediately thanked him and promised. "Well, here is the ham, and now you must go straight to the Dead Man's Hall," said the rich brother, throwing the ham to him.

"Well, I will do what I have promised," said the poor man, and he took the ham and set off. He went on and on all day, and at nightfall he came to a place where there was a bright light. I have no doubt this is the place, thought the man with the ham.

An old man with a long white beard was chopping Yule logs.

"Good evening," said the man with the ham.

"Good evening to you. Where are you going at this late hour?" asked the old man.

"I am going to Dead Man's Hall, if only I am on the right track," answered the poor man.

"Oh, yes, you are right enough, for it is here," said the old man. "When you go inside they will all want to buy your ham, for they don't get much meat to eat there. But you must not sell it unless you can get for it the hand mill which stands behind the door. When you come out again I will teach you how to stop the hand mill, which is useful for almost everything."

So the man with the ham thanked the other for his good advice and rapped at the door. When he went in, everything happened just as the old man had said it would. All the people, great and small, came round him like ants on an anthill, and each tried to outbid the other for the ham.

"By rights my old woman and I should have it for our Christmas dinner, but since you have set your hearts upon it, I must give it up to you," said the man. "But I want in exchange the hand mill standing there behind the door."

At first they would not hear of this, and haggled and bargained with the man, but he stuck to what he had said, and the people were forced to give him the hand mill. When the man came out again into the yard, he asked the old woodcutter how he was to stop the hand mill. And when he

had learned that, he thanked him and set off with all the speed he could, but did not arrive home until after the clock had struck twelve on Christmas Eve.

"Now where in the world have you been?" asked his wife. "Here I have sat waiting, hour after hour, and have not even two sticks to lay across each other under the Christmas porridge pot."

"Oh, I could not come before," said the man. "I had something of importance to see about, and a long way to go, too. But now you shall just see!" Then he set the hand mill on the table, and bade it first grind light, then a tablecloth, and then meat and cakes, and everything else that was good for a Christmas Eve supper.

And the mill ground all that he ordered.

"Bless me!" said the old woman as one thing after another appeared. And she wanted to know where her husband had got the mill, but he would not tell her.

"Never mind where I got it. You can see it is a good one, and the water that turns it will never freeze," said the man. So he ground meat and pastries, and all kinds of good things to last all Christmastide, and on the third day he invited all his friends to come to a feast.

Now when the rich brother saw all there was at the banquet and in the house, he was both vexed and angry, for he grudged everything his brother had. "On Christmas Eve he was so poor he came to me and begged for a trifle, and now he gives a feast as if he were both a count and a king!" thought he. "But, for heaven's sake, tell me where you got your riches," he said to his brother.

"From behind the door," said the man who owned the mill, for he did not choose to satisfy his brother on that point. But later in the evening he could not refrain from telling how he had come by the hand mill. "There you see what has brought me all my wealth!" And he brought out the mill and made it grind first one thing and then another.

When the brother saw that, he insisted on having the mill and after a great deal of persuasion got it. But he had to give three hundred dollars for it, and the poor brother was to keep it till the haymaking was over, for he thought, if I keep it as long as that, I can make it grind food that will last many a long year.

During that time the mill did not grow rusty, and when hay harvest came the rich brother took it, but the other had taken good care not to teach him how to stop it. It was evening when the rich man reached home, and in the morning he bade the old woman who was his housekeeper to go out and spread the hay after the mowers, and he would attend to the house himself that day.

So, when dinner time grew near, he set the mill on the kitchen table and said, "Grind herrings and milk pottage, and do it both quickly and well."

So the mill began to grind herrings and milk pottage, and first all the dishes and tubs were filled, and then the stuff covered the kitchen floor. The man twisted and turned it, and did all he could to make the mill stop, but however he turned and screwed it, the mill went on grinding, and in a short time the pottage rose so high that the man was like to be drowned. So he threw open the parlor door, but it was not long before the mill had ground the parlor full too, and it was with difficulty and danger that the man could go through the stream of pottage and get hold of the door latch. When he got the door open, he did not stay long in the room, but ran out, and the herrings and pottage came after him and streamed out over both farm and field.

Now the old woman, who was out spreading the hay, began to think dinner was long in coming, and she said to the women and the mowers, "Though the master does not call us home, we may as well go. It may be he finds he is not good at making pottage, and I should do well to help him." So they began to straggle homeward, but a little way up the hill they met the herrings and the pottage and bread, all pouring forth and winding about one over the other, and the man himself in front of the flood.

"Would to heaven that each of you had a hundred stomachs! Take care that you are not drowned in the pottage!" he cried as he went by them as if Mischief were at his heels, down to where his brother dwelt. Then he begged him to take the mill back at once, for, said he, "If it grinds one hour more the whole district will be destroyed by herrings and pottage!" But the brother would not take it until the other paid him another three hundred dollars, and that he was obliged to do.

Now the poor brother had both the money and the mill again. So it was not long before he had a farmhouse much finer than his brother's. In fact, the mill ground him so much money that he covered the outside of the house with plates of gold. Since the farmhouse lay close by the seashore, it shone and glittered far out to sea. Everyone who sailed by put in to visit the rich man in the gold farmhouse, and everyone wanted to see the wonderful mill, for the report of it spread far and wide, and there was no one who had not heard of it.

After a long, long time a certain skipper came who wished to see the mill. He asked if it could make salt. "Yes, it can make salt," said the man who owned it, and when the skipper heard that, he wished with all his might and main to have the mill. He thought that if he had it he would not have to sail far away over the perilous sea for freights of salt. At first the man would not hear of parting with it, but the skipper begged and prayed, and at last the man sold it to him for many, many thousands of dollars. When the skipper had the mill he did not stay long, for he was afraid the man would change his mind. He did not even take time to ask how he was to stop it grinding, but went on board his ship as fast as he could.

When he had gone a little way out to sea he took the mill on deck. "Grind salt, and grind both quickly and well," said the skipper. So the mill began to grind salt till it spouted out like water. When the skipper had the ship filled he wanted to stop the mill, but whichever way he turned it and however he tried, it went on grinding, and the heap of salt grew higher and higher, until at last the ship sank.

There lies the mill at the bottom of the sea, and still, day by day, it grinds on: and that is why the sea is salt.

Other titles in this series

Published by

RANDOM HOUSE, 457 MADISON AVENUE, NEW YORK 22, N. Y.

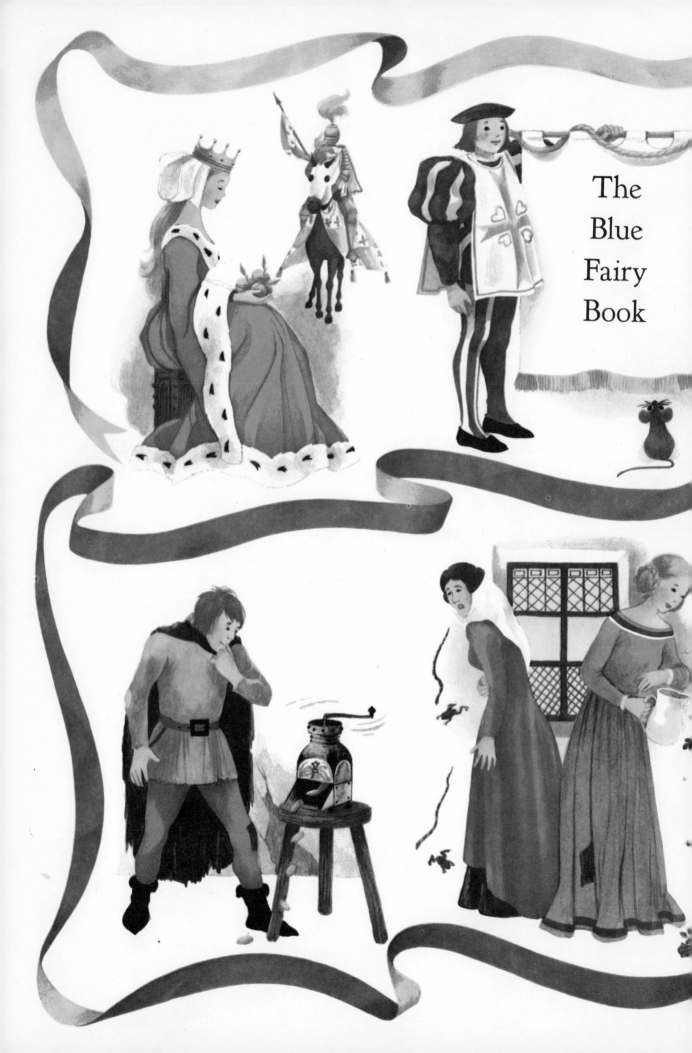

The
Blue
Fairy
Book